Princess Bedtime Stories

Illustrated by the Disney Storybook Art Team

 A GOLDEN BOOK • NEW YORK

rhcbooks.com

ISBN 978-0-7364-3793-6

Printed in the United States of America

10 9 8 7 6 5 4 3 2 1

Disney
PRINCESS
THE LITTLE MERMAID
Ariel's Night Lights

One evening, Princess Ariel and Prince Eric were eating dessert on their balcony. Ariel loved nighttime on land—it was so different from the sea!

"The only lights under the sea are glowing jellyfish and a little bit of moonlight," said Ariel. "There are no torches or lanterns. There's no fire at all!"

"I bet there are no fireflies, either," said Eric. He blew
out the torches. Now the balcony was in total darkness.
Suddenly, some bright sparks zipped through the air.
"Those fireflies are lovely," said Ariel. "They're like
tiny stars that have come to live on land—just like I did!"
Eric agreed.

"Speaking of stars," added Ariel, "I wish we could see more of them here. I used to see so many stars when I snuck up to the surface of the ocean. But now there's so much light coming from the palace, they're hard to see. I know—let's go where we can see *all* the stars!"

Soon Ariel and Eric were in a carriage riding away from the castle. The farther they traveled, the darker the night grew.

When they reached the top of a large hill,
the sky was full of stars.

"This is so beautiful!" said Ariel.

Suddenly, a star shot across the sky, followed
by another and another. It was a meteor shower!
"Amazing!" exclaimed Ariel.
Ariel and Eric would always remember their
beautiful night beneath the stars.

POCAHONTAS

Lost and Found

One evening, Pocahontas was out on the river in her canoe when her best friend, Nakoma, called her back to shore.

"A bad storm is coming!" Nakoma warned. But Pocahontas was enjoying the water with her friends Meeko and Flit. Nakoma ran off to warn the others.

Pocahontas stayed in her canoe and soon
fell asleep. Meeko and Flit did, too.

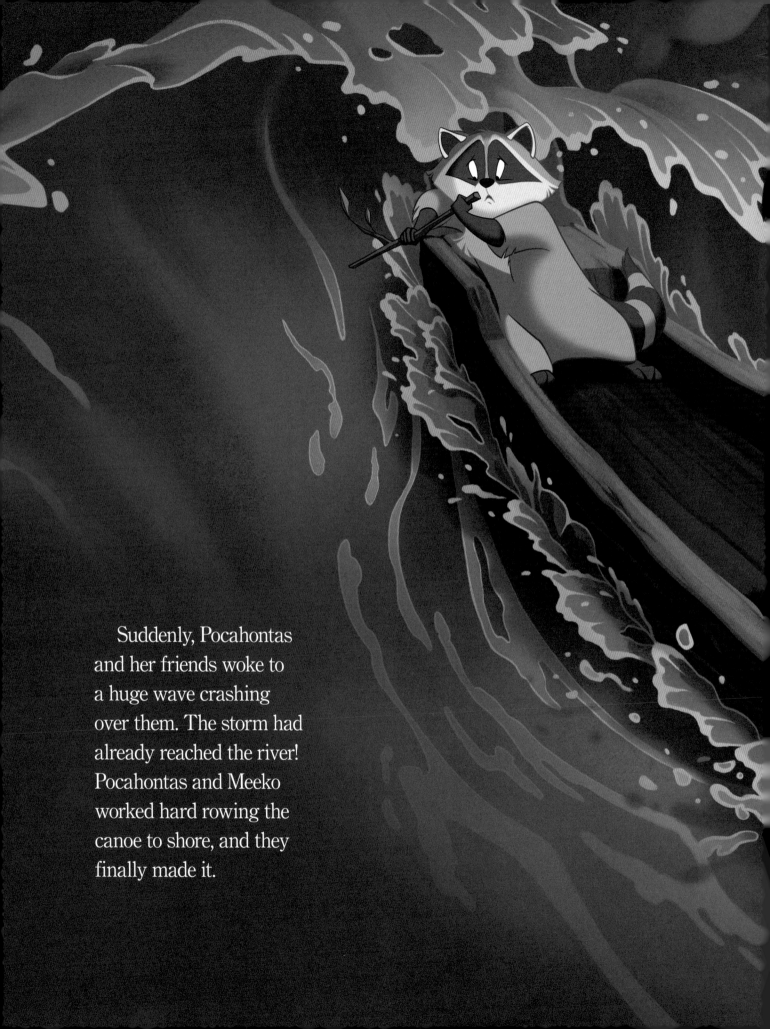

Suddenly, Pocahontas
and her friends woke to
a huge wave crashing
over them. The storm had
already reached the river!
Pocahontas and Meeko
worked hard rowing the
canoe to shore, and they
finally made it.

The friends hurried to the village to prepare
for the storm.

But when Pocahontas got to her father's tent,
she realized that Nakoma hadn't returned from
warning the others!

Worried, Pocahontas ran out into the storm.
"I have to find her!" she called to her father.

Pocahontas looked everywhere. "Nakoma!" She called her friend's name over and
over, but there was no sign of her, until—
"Pocahontas!" The voice was faint, but
it was definitely Nakoma's.

Pocahontas followed her friend's voice until
she found her huddled against a rock.
"I'm so glad you found me!" said Nakoma.
"I was so focused on warning everyone else
that I got lost in the rain and wind."
"I'm glad I found you, too!" said Pocahontas.

She put her arm around Nakoma, and the friends
set out for home. The storm didn't seem so bad now
that they weren't alone.

Soon Pocahontas and Nakoma safely reached Chief
Powhatan's tent. They snuggled by the fire as the
chief told stories about other big storms. Before long,
the friends drifted off to sleep, happy to be together.

Beauty and the Beast

Belle and Chip's Star Story

he evening, Belle and Chip were taking a walk through the castle gardens when Belle pointed out a constellation in the dark sky.

"What's a constellation?" asked Chip.

"It's a group of stars that looks like a picture," explained Belle. "See? Those stars together form the shape of a dragon."

"Cool!" said Chip. "Can we see more constellations?"

Belle took Chip up to a castle balcony, but by then the sky had grown cloudy.

"I'm sorry," said Belle. "We won't be able to see any more constellations tonight."

Chip was disappointed. Belle got an idea.

"We can make our own constellation!" she said. "I know where we can start."

Belle and Chip went to see Wardrobe.

"Do you have anything sparkly or shiny we can borrow?"
asked Belle.

Wardrobe opened her drawers to reveal shiny buttons
and sparkly beads. They would make perfect stars.

"Take as many as you need!" she said.

Next, Belle and Chip found Cogsworth.
"Can we borrow some gears?" asked Chip
excitedly. "They'll make great planets!"
Cogsworth opened a box and gave the
friends several shiny round gears.

"Now we need something to string our stars and planets together," said Belle.

"Maybe Mama has something we can use," Chip said.

She and Chip went to see Mrs. Potts, who gave them an old egg basket.

"You can unravel it for the wire," said Mrs. Potts.

Belle and Chip worked hard stringing their
constellations together. Then Belle asked the
Beast to hang them in the library and cover
them with a large curtain.

Once everything was set, Belle and Chip gathered their friends in the library.

"We have a surprise for you!" Chip said. "A star story!"

The excited friends settled in to listen.

"Once upon a time," Chip began, "a girl got lost in the dark woods. It started to snow."

Belle scattered paper snowflakes through the air.

"Suddenly, a pack of wolves began to chase her!" Chip continued. "The girl ran through the woods, terrified, until out of nowhere, the Beast appeared and fought off the vicious wolves. He threw one of the wolves so far into the sky that it went up, up, up and turned into a constellation forever. To this day, it is a reminder to the wolves not to hurt the Beast's friends!"

As Chip finished the story, Belle pulled away the curtain to reveal their constellation. The friends clapped and cheered.

"Wait!" said Lumiere. "You're forgetting one important detail. The stars must shine!" He pointed his candles at the constellation, and every bead and button sparkled. Belle and Chip's star story was complete!

DISNEY PRINCESS
Cinderella
Good Night, Gus-Gus

It was almost bedtime, and Cinderella's mouse friends
needed to get ready for bed. But Gus had never lived in
a house, so he had never gotten ready for bed before!

"I'll show you how," said Cinderella. "First, I have a

She held up a pair of pajamas she had made.
"For me?" Gus was excited. "Thank you, Cinderelly!"

Gus tried on his new pajamas. They fit perfectly! He showed them to the rest of the mice. "Gus-Gus loves pajamas!" he said. "Gus-Gus wear pajamas all the time!"

Next, Cinderella told Gus how to brush his teeth.

Gus loved the foamy mint toothpaste. "Mmm," he said.

But when Cinderella gave him a bar of soap, he didn't know what to do with it.

"Now you wash your face—like this," said his friends, and they showed him how.

Once the mice were all clean and ready, Cinderella kissed them good night, and Suzy tucked them into their little mouse beds. "This is so cozy!" said Gus as he settled under the covers. Then Cinderella told them a bedtime story.

Soon all the mice were fast asleep.
Cinderella tiptoed to her bed and got
under the covers.
Within minutes, she was asleep, too.
It was hard work getting mice ready for bed!